SQUAREHEAD

Story by Harriet Ziefert

SQUAREHEAD

Paintings by Todd McKie

HOUGHTON MIFFLIN COMPANY BOSTON 2001

Walter Lorraine Books

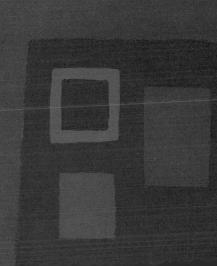

For Meridyth Moses,
who made the introduction
H. Z.

For Judy
T. M.

Walter Lorraine ⟨wn⟩ Books

Text copyright 2001 by Harriet Ziefert
Illustrations copyright 2001 by Todd McKie

Library of Congress Cataloging-in-Publication Data

Ziefert, Harriet.
 Squarehead / written by Harriet Ziefert ; illustrated by Todd McKie.
   p. cm.
 Summary: George only likes things that are square like himself until a
dream reminds him of how nice round can be.
   ISBN 0-618-08378-2
   [1. Self-perception Fiction. 2. Shape Fiction. 3. Square Fiction. 4.
   Circle Fiction.]
I. McKie, Todd, 1944- II. Title.

PZ7.Z487 Sr 2001
[E] dc21   00-057508

Printed in China for Harriet Ziefert, Inc.
HZI 10 9 8 7 6 5 4 3 2 1

George was a squarehead,
a box from cheek to cheek.

George disliked circles, ovals and spheres.

Snowballs gave him shivers.

Eggs made him sick.

Baseballs could be dangerous.

Wheels were annoying.

"The world is square!"
George announced.

"There are square cats...

square dogs...

square birds...

and square people. I like everything and

everyone that's shaped like me!"

When George fell asleep at night,
he even had square dreams—

where bright-colored creatures
danced and floated and swam

through his mind...,

until the night George's dream
carried him out of his world
and far away to outer space.

Circling, circling,
circling through space,

a curved moon...

a ringed planet...

a satellite sphere...

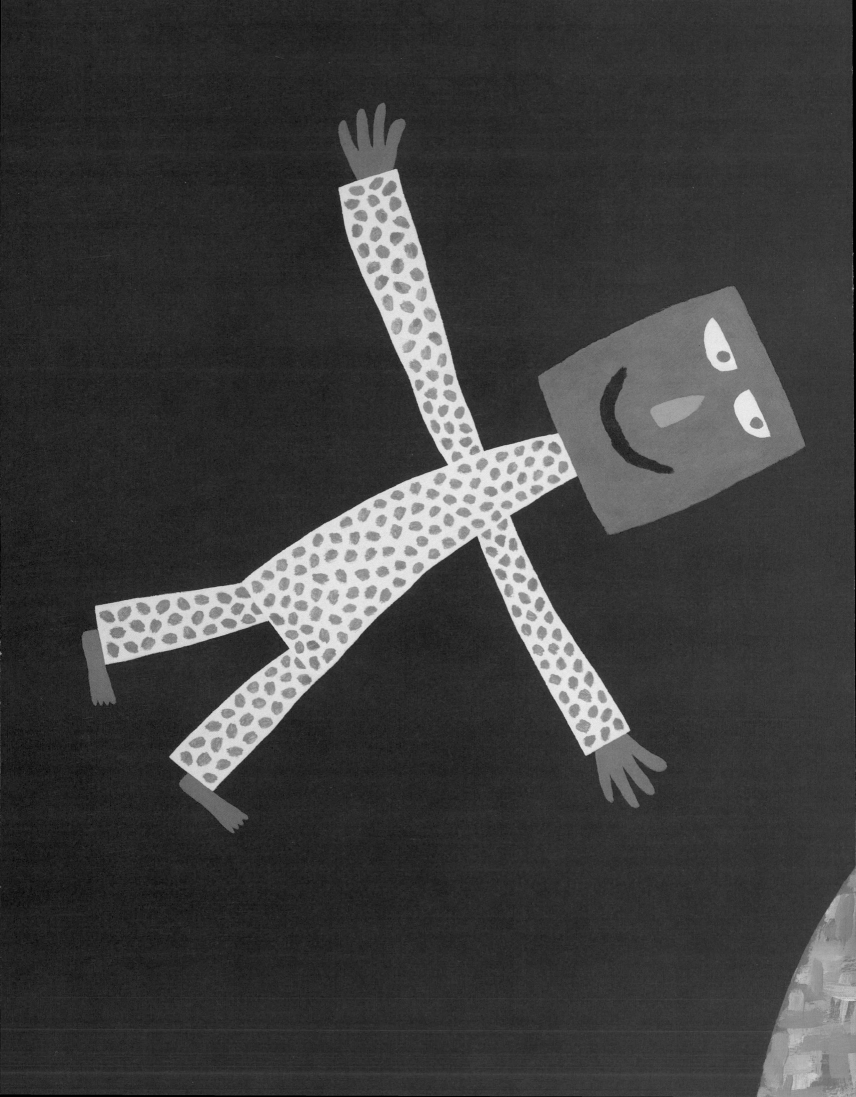

and the earth big and round.

"Round is awesome," he said.

"Round is neat.
The sun is round...

and so is the world!"